WEIRD AND UNUSUAL ANIMALS

JAPANESE SPIDER CRABS

by Wendy Perkins

I0895010

AMICUS HIGH INTEREST • AMICUS INK

Amicus High Interest and
Amicus Ink are imprints of Amicus
P.O. Box 1329, Mankato, MN 56002
www.amicuspublishing.us

Library of Congress Cataloging-in-Publication Data
Names: Perkins, Wendy, 1957- author.
Title: Japanese spider crabs / by Wendy Perkins.
Description: Mankato, Minnesota : Amicus High Interest, [2018] Series: Weird and unusual animals | Audience: K to grade 3. | Includes bibliographical references and index.
Identifiers: LCCN 2016038827| ISBN 9781681511580 (library binding) | ISBN 9781681521893 (pbk.) | ISBN 9781681512488 (ebook)
Subjects: LCSH: Spider crabs--Juvenile literature. | Crabs--Juvenile literature.
Classification: LCC QL444.M33 P47525 2018 | DDC 595.3/86--dc23
LC record available at https://lccn.loc.gov/2016038827

Photo Credits: f11photo/Shutterstock cover, 8-9; Franco Banfi/Getty 2; Leonid Serebrennikov/Alamy Stock Photo 4-5; Project1photography/Dreamstime.com 6-7; Tom McHugh 11; Scenics & Science/Alamy Stock Photo 13; anopdesignstock/iStock 14; Ethan Daniels/Shutterstock 16-17; Mark Conlin/Alamy Stock Photo 18-19; Rebekah D. Wallace, University of Georgia/InsectImages.org 20-21; SeaPics 22

Editor: Wendy Dieker
Designer: Aubrey Harper
Photo Researchers: Aubrey Harper and Holly Young

Printed in the United States of America

HC 10 9 8 7 6 5 4 3 2 1
PB 10 9 8 7 6 5 4 3 2 1

TABLE OF CONTENTS

THE BIGGEST CRAB

Giant crabs live deep in the ocean near Japan. One kind has a body as big as a basketball. It is the largest kind of crab in the world. It is a Japanese spider crab.

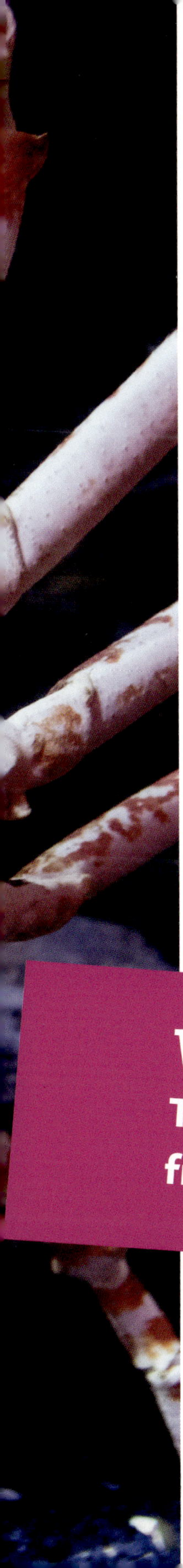

SPIDERY LEGS

Spider crabs get their name from their legs. Just like a spider, these crabs have long thin legs.

Weird but True

These crabs have ten legs. The two front legs are claws.

LEGGY CRABS

The Japanese spider crab's body stops growing when it is an **adult**. But their legs grow and grow. They can each be as long as a couch! Wow!

Sea Walker

Hooks on the tips of the crab's legs grip rocks. Japanese spider crabs don't swim. They walk on the bottom of the ocean.

Weird but True

If a spider crab's leg breaks off, it can grow a new one.

BABY CRABS

A female crab lays a million eggs. The eggs hatch after ten days. A baby crab is called a **larva**. At first, the larva floats in the ocean. After a month, it sinks to the sandy sea bottom.

Weird but True
A spider crab egg is about the size of the head of a pin.

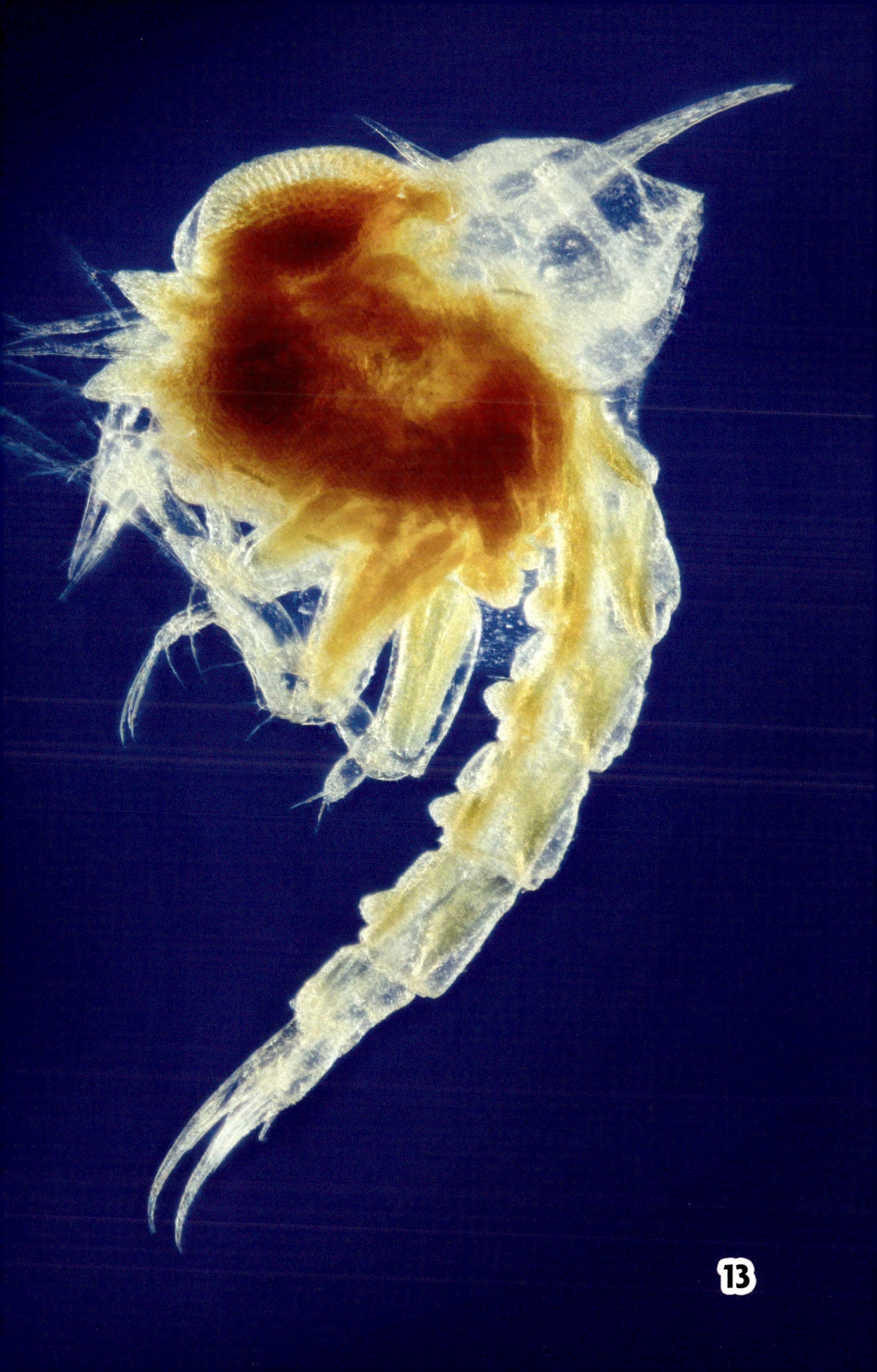

OFF WITH THE OLD

As a crab grows, it **molts**. It sheds its shell. The shell pops open in the back. The crab crawls out. It hides until the new shell turns hard.

Weird but True

It can take two days for the crab to molt.

CRAZY COVER UP

A crab's hard shell keeps it safe. But small, young spider crabs must be careful. They stick **sea sponges** and seaweed on their shell. It helps them hide.

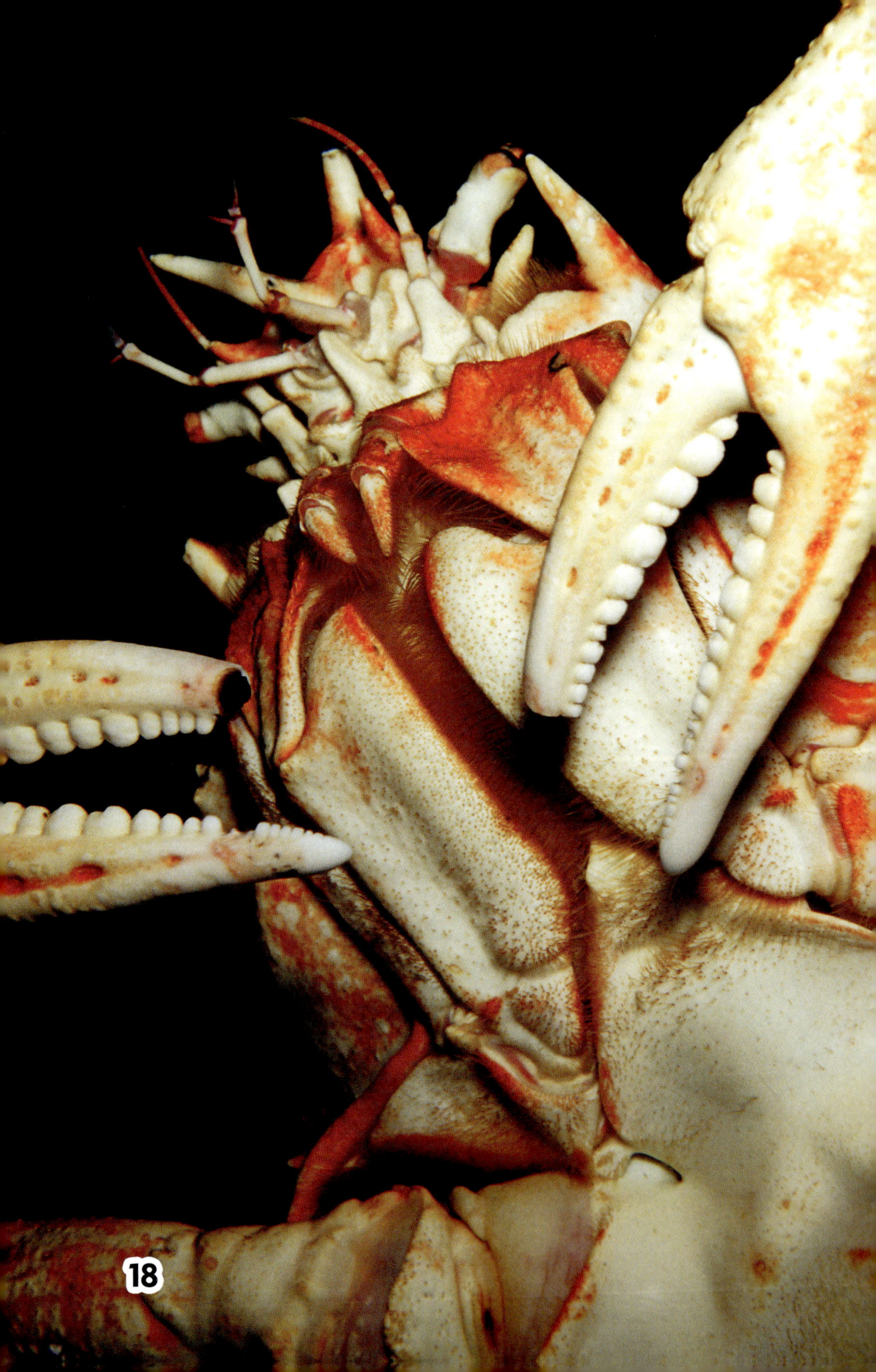

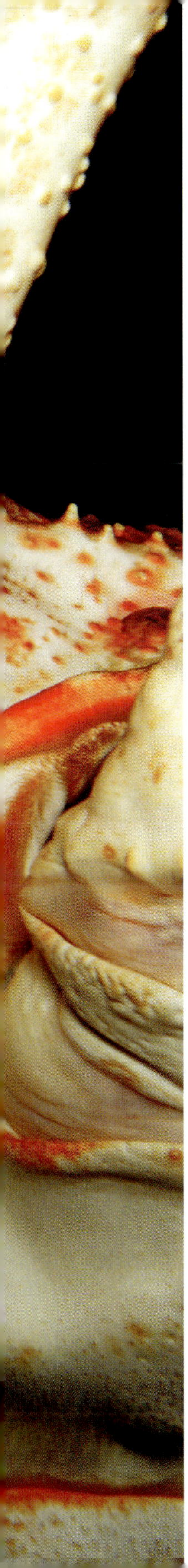

MEAL TIME

Spider crabs find food on the ocean floor. They use their claws to pinch off pieces of dead animals. They also eat bits of seaweed. Crabs help keep the sea clean.

CRAB PARADE

Japanese spider crabs are big. They are weird. But they don't hurt people. Each spring, they gather in shallow water to find **mates**. It's a crab parade!

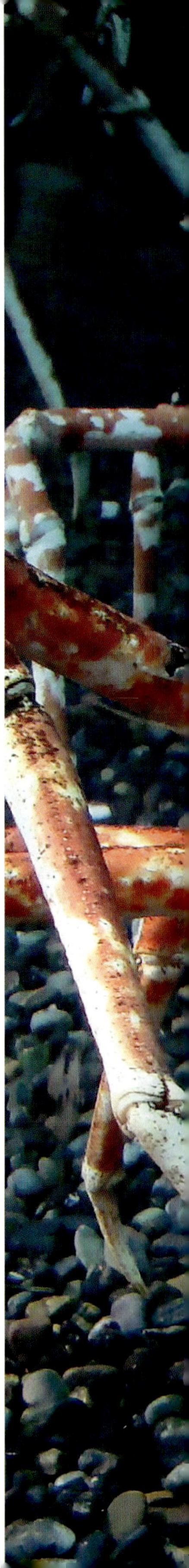

A LOOK AT JAPANESE SPIDER CRABS

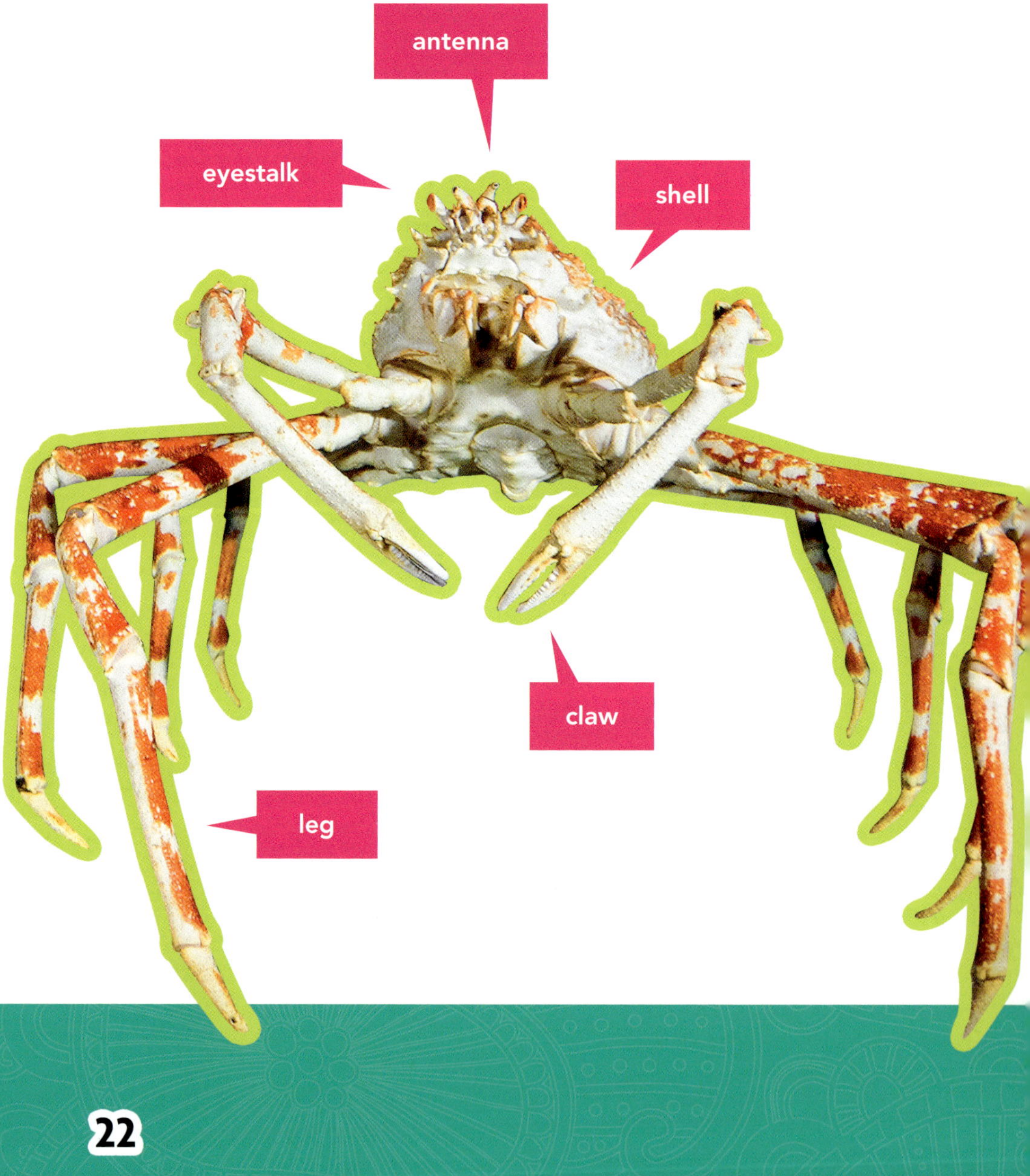

WORDS TO KNOW

adult – an animal that is fully grown

larva – a crab that has just hatched from its egg

mate – a male or female partner needed to make baby crabs

molt – to shed the outer shell as the crab grows

sea sponge – a simple animal that grows on the ocean floor; sea sponges have a rubbery skeleton with holes that take in water.

LEARN MORE

Books

Bodden, Valerie. *Crabs*. Mankato, Minn.: Creative Education, 2017.

Nagelhout, Ryan. *Crabs*. New York: Gareth Stevens Pub., 2013.

Websites

Kids Discover: Japanese Spider Crabs
http://www.kidsdiscover.com/quick-reads/japanese-spider-crabs-twelve-feet-legs/

Tennessee Aquarium: Giant Japanese Spider Crab
www.tnaqua.org/our-animals/invertebrates/giant-japanese-spider-crab

INDEX

Every effort has been made to ensure that these websites are appropriate for children. However, because of the nature of the Internet, it is impossible to guarantee that these sites will remain active indefinitely or that their contents will not be altered.